THE STORY ABOUT ME

Miriam Schlein is the author of more than ninety books for children, among them the much-loved *The Way Mothers Are*. She lives in New York City. Many of her books have been included in textbooks and translated into other languages.

Kristina Stephenson has worked as a set and costume designer for the theater and for children's television. She began illustrating books for children after her daughter was born. She now lives in Salisbury, England, with her musician husband and two children.

THE STORY ABOUT ME

Miriam Schlein

Illustrated by Kristina Stephenson

Albert Whitman & Company
Morton Grove, Illinois

Library of Congress Cataloging-in-Publication Data
is available from the Library of Congress.

For more information about Albert Whitman & Company, please
visit our web site at www.albertwhitman.com.

This book is for Katherine and Laura,
who turned out to be my double Grandma-cup birthday gift.—M.S.

For my parents, whose never-ending love for
each other will always be my inspiration.—K.S.

I have a grandma who loves to tell me stories all about our family.

"Do you have a story today, Grandma?"
I asked her.

She nodded.

Uncle John and Mom as kids

Grandma, when she was a girl

Cousin Milton

Mom and Dad

It was a silly question.
Because she never runs out of stories.

Grandma's dad with his first car

Grandma's dad and his friends

Grandma with her dad and mom (my great-grandparents)

Sometimes they're about people I don't even know.
Because the stories happened so long ago.

"Do I know the people in the story?"
I asked her.

Grandma smiled.
"This story," she said, "is about *you*."

We settled down in her big chair,
and she began.

"It was my birthday," Grandma said.
"Your mama handed me a present.

'Happy birthday, Mom,' she said.

I opened the package.
It was this cup."

She held up her special cup–
the one that says GRANDMA on it.

"It was your mama's way of telling me
you were going to be born.
Wow! Was I excited!
I was going to become a grandma.

But it didn't happen right away.
We had to wait for you to arrive.

We waited. And waited.
Days and days and more days went by.

You sure took your time to get here!

While he waited,
your daddy composed
a special song
for you on his guitar.

Your great-uncle Paul
kept calling on the phone from Washington, D.C.,
saying, 'Well? Well?
When is she coming?
When will it be?'

Your great-aunt Sally knitted you
a sweater, and leggings, and a hat.
All very small.

And your Uncle John?
He didn't know what to do
to get ready to be an uncle.
He was never an uncle before!

So he just waited.
It's not easy waiting.

And all the while, your mama's belly
got bigger and rounder
as you grew bigger inside her.

As we waited, we began to get busy.
There was lots to do
to get ready for you.

All over the country,
people were waiting for you.

Your big cousin Kristen
waited for you out in Idaho.
She was eager to take you hiking.

Your second-cousin Willie
was waiting for you
in Kalamazoo,
with a new kazoo,
so he could play duets with you.

And your first-cousin-twice-removed,
Milton the dentist,
said, 'Where is she?
I'm ready to fix her teeth.'
He was joking.
He knew when you were a little baby,
just born,
you wouldn't even have any teeth.

You know, you caused quite a commotion
all over the place
        for such a little person
            who wasn't even born yet.

But I'll tell you,
when you finally got here,
the commotion didn't die down.
There was even a bigger commotion.
Not only did you arrive,
EVERYBODY arrived!

They came from
all over the place.

They came by bus,

they came by train,

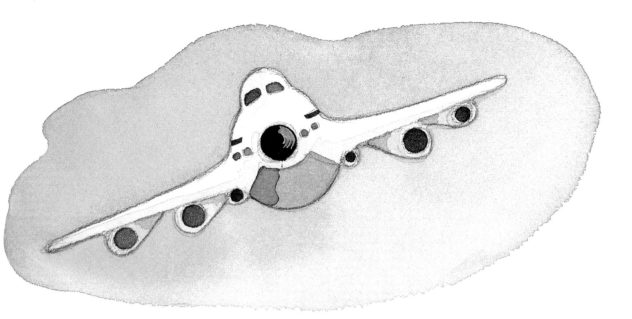

they came by plane,

they came by car. . .

just to see you.

And what was there to see?
A little round face,
not much hair,
little tiny legs,
tiny little fingers
on tiny little hands.

And, funny little thing that you were,
right away, we all loved you so much!"

"Why, Grandma? Why did you love me?
You didn't even know me yet."

"Why?
I don't know.
That's just the way it is with families."